Rat Naps

Written by Paul Shipton
Illustrated by Tomislav Zlatic

Sid is a rat at the tip.

Sid naps in a sock.

Tim naps in a tin.

Cam naps in a cup.

Rick is not a rat! Rick is a cat!

Rick pads up.

Rick runs at the rats.

Run, rats, run!

Did Rick get a rat?

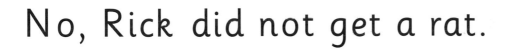

No, Rick did not get a rat.

Rick got a sock!

Rick is mad.

The tip

🐾 Ideas for reading 🐾

Written by Clare Dowdall BA(Ed), MA(Ed)
Lecturer and Primary Literacy Consultant

Learning objectives: read simple words by sounding out and blending the phonemes all through the word from left to right; read some high frequency words; read a range of familiar and common words and simple sentences independently; retell narratives in the correct sequence, drawing on the language patterns of stories; use phonic knowledge to write simple regular words and make phonetically plausible attempts at more complex words

Curriculum links: Creative Development: Use their imagination in art and design, music, dance, imaginative and role-play and stories

Focus phonemes: s, a, d, t, p, i, n, r, ck, o, m, c, u, g, e

Fast words: the, no

Word count: 61

Getting started

- Write the names, *Sid, Tim, Cam, Rick* on the whiteboard and ask children to blend the sounds out loud to read them. Tell them that these are the names of the characters in the book.

- Look at the front cover together and read the title. Ask children to describe what is happening in the picture: *Where is the rat? What is he doing? What is a nap? What is going to happen?*

Reading and responding

- Ask children to read independently to p7. Invite children to demonstrate how they can blend new words.

- Pause at p7. Ask children to recount events so far and to suggest what might happen next.

- Ask children to continue to read independently to p13. Move around the group encouraging and praising children who are blending and rereading whole sentences for fluency.

- Invite fast-finishers to reread the story aloud to a partner with expression, using punctuation to help them.